WISCONSIN

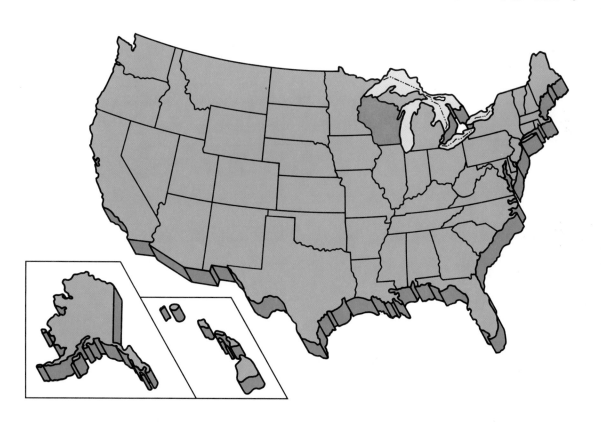

WISCONSIN

Gretchen Bratvold

Lerner Publications Company

LIBRARY OF CONGRESS
CATALOGING-IN-PUBLICATION DATA
Bratvold, Gretchen.
    Wisconsin / Gretchen Bratvold.
      p.   cm. — (Hello USA)
    Includes index.
    Summary: Introduces the geography, history, people, industries, and other highlights of Wisconsin.
    ISBN 0-8225-2700-6 (lib. bdg.)
    1. Wisconsin—Juvenile literature.
[1. Wisconsin.] I. Title. II. Series.
F581.3.B73 1991
977.5—dc20   90-39327
                             CIP
                             AC

Manufactured in the United States of America
1 2 3 4 5 6 7 8 9 10 99 98 97 96 95 94 93 92 91

Cover photograph by Action USA, Cy White.

The glossary that begins on page 68 gives definitions of words shown in **bold type** in the text.

 This book is printed on recycled paper.

CONTENTS

Did You Know...?

☐ The name *Wisconsin* may mean "gathering of the waters" or "place of the beaver." The word comes from the French version of an Ojibwa Indian term.

☐ The famous Ringling Brothers Circus first performed in Baraboo, Wisconsin, in 1884. The company still tours the country, and its posters, wagons, and equipment are displayed at the Circus World Museum in Baraboo.

In 1887 William Horlick, from Racine, Wisconsin, made the first malted milk.

A Wisconsin paper manufacturer invented and sold the world's first facial tissues in 1917. The product was advertised as an easy, disposable way to wipe off makeup. Imagine the company's surprise when it learned that its customers were using the tissues, called Kleenex, to blow their noses!

Wisconsin's dairy cows produce 3 billion gallons (11 billion liters) of milk each year—more than any other state. That's enough to fill a nine-foot-deep (three-meter-deep) Olympic-size swimming pool almost 11 times a day.

Wisconsin is famous for its dairy cattle.

A Trip
Around the State

With hundreds of dairy farms, Wisconsin produces more milk than any other state in the country. For this reason, the rolling hills, fertile plains and valleys, and thousands of lakes that cover Wisconsin have come to be called America's Dairyland.

Glaciers carved out the basin for Lake Superior and left rocks and boulders along the shore.

Seventy-thousand years ago, during the last **Ice Age**, enormous sheets of ice called **glaciers** covered a large part of North America. As the glaciers inched their way through the Great Lakes region, they ground away soil and rocks and shaped the land we now know as Wisconsin.

The state has four main land regions, and glaciers carved three of them—the Northern Highland, the Central Plain, and the Eastern Ridges and Lowlands. The fourth region, the Western Upland, was untouched by the glaciers.

Wisconsin is located in the upper midwestern area of the United States. The state has four neighbors—Michigan, Illinois, Iowa, and Minnesota. The Mississippi River runs along much of the western border. Two huge lakes, Superior and Michigan, also form part of Wisconsin's boundaries. These bodies of water belong to the five Great Lakes of North America.

The Northern Highland expands across most of northern Wisconsin. Glaciers in this region hollowed out basins that later filled with water. They also left behind mounds of earth and stones. These rocky hills are called **moraines**. The state's highest point, Timms Hill, rises to 1,952 feet (595 m) in the Northern Highland.

South of the highland region lies the Central Plain, which has both level and hilly land. Low, flat terrain stretches across the southern end of the Central Plain. Thousands of years ago, water covered this part of the region.

The Eastern Ridges and Lowlands spread across much of eastern Wisconsin. Rich deposits of

Swimmers jump from sandstone cliffs into the Wisconsin River at the Wisconsin Dells.

12

earth left behind by the glaciers make this gently rolling region the most fertile in the state.

Glaciers did not pass through Wisconsin's fourth region. For this reason, the Western Upland has more rugged terrain than other areas of the state. Limestone and sandstone **bluffs** rise from the banks of the Mississippi River in the southwestern corner of the region.

The gently rolling land of the Eastern Ridges and Lowlands is good for growing crops such as corn.

A loon rests in the brush beside one of Wisconsin's many lakes.

Wisconsin has many rivers. In the western half of the state, the Wisconsin, Chippewa, and St. Croix rivers flow into the great Mississippi. In the east, the Wolf and Fox rivers and many smaller streams empty into Lake Michigan. Hundreds of waterfalls spill over steep drops along these rivers.

Long ago, when the glaciers melted, water collected in the hollows the ice had gouged out of the earth. As a result, Wisconsin has more than 8,000 natural lakes, mostly in the north. Green Lake is the deepest, and Lake Winnebago is the largest.

For most of Wisconsin, summer temperatures average about 70° F (21° C). The far north, however, is about 10° F (5° C) cooler. Winters are often long and cold throughout the state, with temperatures plunging far below 0° F (−18° C) in the northwest. Along the shores of Lakes Superior and Michigan, breezes from the water warm the air in the winter and cool it in the summer.

During winter, some Wisconsinites enjoy playing in the snow.

Because plenty of rain and snow fall in Wisconsin, the state has lush plant life during the warmer months. Thunderstorms and occasional tornadoes pass through the region in the spring and summer.

Forests shade much of the northern half of Wisconsin. But many open fields stretch across the south. Early settlers cleared the trees from this area so they could farm the rich soil. Wildflowers and shrubs such as blueberry, Juneberry, and huckleberry also grow in Wisconsin.

A baby white-tailed deer peeps through greenery *(left)*. Wisconsin's state animal, the badger *(below)*, is an expert at tunneling through the ground.

Many white-tailed deer scamper through Wisconsin's forests, where black bears, coyotes, and foxes also roam. Excellent swimmers, Wisconsin's minks, beavers, and muskrats splash in the state's rivers and lakes. Skunks and badgers burrow underground.

Wisconsin's Story

During the Ice Age, land connected the North American and Asian continents at what is now the Bering Strait. Hunters from Asia followed herds of animals across this long bridge of land and entered America. By 6000 B.C., Asians had settled in various parts of North and South America. These people and their descendants are called Indians, or Native Americans.

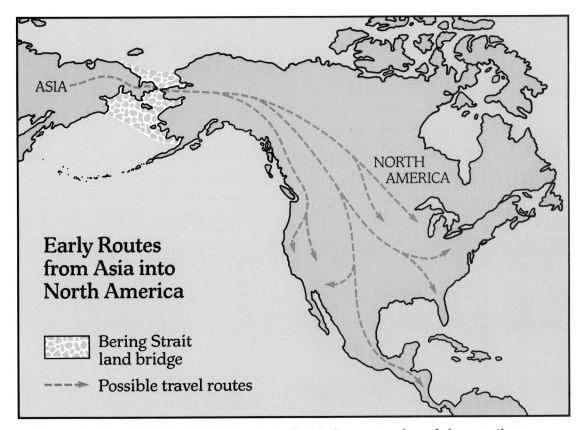

Early Routes from Asia into North America

Bering Strait land bridge

- - - → Possible travel routes

ASIA

NORTH AMERICA

Many scientists think that North America's first Indians came from Asia more than 40,000 years ago. Some of them eventually settled in what is now Wisconsin.

The Indians who moved into the region that is now Wisconsin came sometime after 10,000 B.C., when the last glaciers in the area had melted. Some of the newcomers were the Winnebago, Dakota, and Menominee.

The Indians hunted and fished, and they grew a few crops—especially corn, beans, and squash. Some of them went out in canoes to gather wild rice, which grew in shallow water. They used bark and brush to build homes, and they buried their dead in large mounds of earth shaped like birds, bears, and other animals.

The Menominee Indians speared fish at night with the aid of torchlights. The bright flames lured fish to the surface of the water.

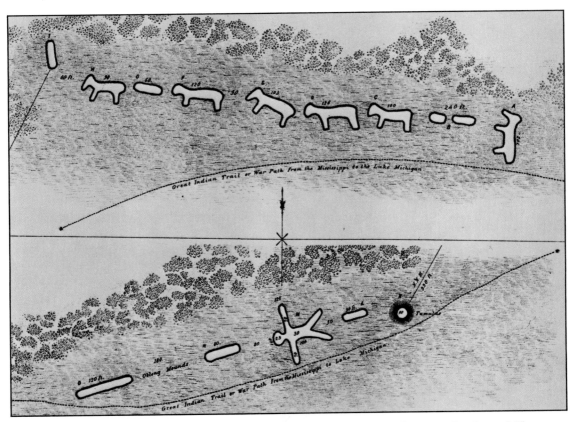

Hundreds of years ago, Wisconsin's Indians buried their dead in mounds shaped like huge animals. Some of the mounds were over 100 feet (30 m) long.

Ojibwa Indians harvested wild rice growing in shallow lake water.

In the 1600s, many other Indian groups—including the Sauk, Fox, Kickapoo, and Potawatomi—arrived in Wisconsin from the east. Some came to escape unfriendly Europeans who had settled along the East Coast. Others sought safety from warring Indians.

The first Europeans to set foot in Wisconsin probably did not reach the area until the 1620s. Coming from eastern Canada, the French explorer Jean Nicolet sailed through the Great Lakes and landed on the shore of Green Bay in 1634. At first he thought he had found a water route to China.

With his beard and white skin, Nicolet looked very strange to the Native Americans who greeted

When Jean Nicolet greeted Wisconsin's Indians in 1634, he wore a Chinese robe because he thought he had landed in China.

him, and he was surprised to find Indians when he had expected Chinese people. Disappointed, Nicolet returned to his home in Canada. He had learned what the Native Americans already knew— North America was a huge chunk of land.

James Marquette worked as a missionary
for the Catholic Church in Wisconsin.

WISCONSIN'S TRIBUTE.

JAMES MARQUETTE S. J.,
WHO, WITH LOUIS JOLIET
DISCOVERED THE MISSISSIPPI RIVER
AT PRAIRIE DU CHIEN, WIS.,
JUNE 17, 1673.

More French people—especially Roman Catholic **missionaries** and fur traders—came from Canada in the mid-1600s. The missionaries wanted to teach the Indians the Christian religion. The fur traders depended on the hunting skills of the Indians, who were experts at trapping and skinning animals.

For their work, the Indians received European goods such as mirrors, knives, guns, iron pots, glassware, and alcohol. Beaver coats and hats were fashionable in Europe, so beaver pelts sold for high prices.

Gradually, the Indians became more dependent on the goods they got from the fur traders. The traders then made the Indians bring in more and more pelts to trade for the items they wanted.

An Indian meets a French fur trader.

During the 1700s, boatmen carried both furs and trade goods between Indian and French Canadian settlements. After paddling all day, the men camped along rocky shores.

For many decades, the Indians and French lived together peacefully. Eventually, however, trouble arose over control of the Fox and Wisconsin rivers. The Fox Indians and the French each relied on these waterways for travel. In 1712 war erupted. Battles continued for 28 years, until the French overpowered the Fox.

The war made other Indian groups besides the Fox angry with the French. Without the support of these Indians, French strength in the region weakened.

Between 1754 and 1763, during the French and Indian War, the French fought against the British for North American territory. Some Indians sided with the French in this war. But the British defeated the French, and Wisconsin passed to British control.

British rule did not last long, however. After Britain lost the American revolutionary war (1775–1783), Wisconsin became part of the territory of the United States. By this time, many of the Indians in Wisconsin had died. Many had been killed in battles during the 1700s, and others had caught deadly diseases from the white people.

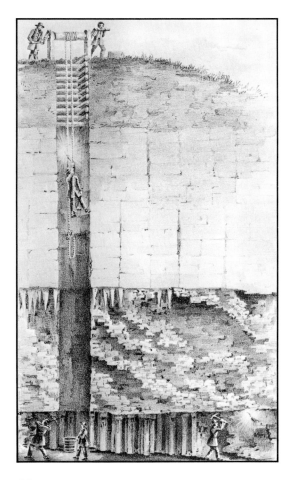

Lead miners were lowered down narrow shafts that led to underground mines.

In the 1820s, more white people began moving into southwestern Wisconsin because it had rich deposits of lead. These settlers built permanent towns and mined the lead, which was needed to make paint and other products.

As the demand for lead increased, many miners came to Wisconsin. Some of the miners lived in caves that they dug into

Wisconsin's first miners found lead near the ground's surface when they dug into the sides of hills.

the hillsides. These people were called "Badgers," because, like the animal, they burrowed shelters in- to the earth. Eventually, Badger became a nickname for all Wisconsinites.

The U.S. government made Indians give up some of their land in southwestern Wisconsin at this meeting at Prairie du Chien in 1825.

In 1832 a Sauk Indian chief named Black Hawk led 1,000 Indians across the Mississippi River from Iowa into Illinois to regain farmland taken over by the white settlers. Thinking that the Indians were going to war, the settlers called out their troops. The Indians fled to Wisconsin and fought back, but they were greatly outnumbered. Nearly all of Black Hawk's people were killed.

30

After the Black Hawk War, there were no more Indian wars in Wisconsin, and U.S. officials made the Indians sign **treaties** giving up control of their territory. By 1848 the United States had gotten legal claim to all of the land in the region. That same year, Wisconsin became the 30th state to join the Union.

Wisconsin's first flag was designed in 1863. The version shown here became official in 1981, when the state's name and its year of admission into the Union were added.

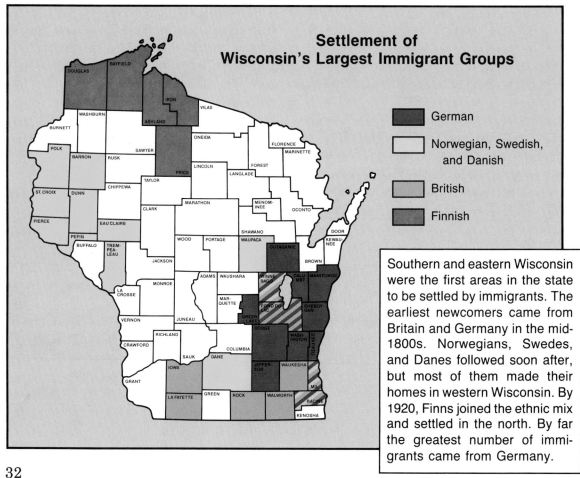

Settlement of Wisconsin's Largest Immigrant Groups

Legend:
- German
- Norwegian, Swedish, and Danish
- British
- Finnish

Counties labeled on map: DOUGLAS, BAYFIELD, IRON, VILAS, WASHBURN, ASHLAND, BURNETT, ONEIDA, FLORENCE, MARINETTE, POLK, SAWYER, BARRON, RUSK, LINCOLN, FOREST, LANGLADE, TAYLOR, ST. CROIX, CHIPPEWA, DUNN, CLARK, MARATHON, MENOMINEE, OCONTO, PIERCE, EAU CLAIRE, PEPIN, BUFFALO, TREMPEALEAU, WOOD, PORTAGE, WAUPACA, SHAWANO, DOOR, KEWAUNEE, JACKSON, OUTAGAMIE, BROWN, MONROE, ADAMS, WAUSHARA, WINNEBAGO, CALUMET, MANITOWOC, LA CROSSE, MARQUETTE, FOND DU LAC, SHEBOYGAN, VERNON, JUNEAU, GREEN LAKE, DODGE, RICHLAND, COLUMBIA, WASHINGTON, OZAUKEE, CRAWFORD, SAUK, DANE, JEFFERSON, WAUKESHA, IOWA, MIL(WAUKEE), GRANT, LA FAYETTE, GREEN, ROCK, WALWORTH, RACINE, KENOSHA

Southern and eastern Wisconsin were the first areas in the state to be settled by immigrants. The earliest newcomers came from Britain and Germany in the mid-1800s. Norwegians, Swedes, and Danes followed soon after, but most of them made their homes in western Wisconsin. By 1920, Finns joined the ethnic mix and settled in the north. By far the greatest number of immigrants came from Germany.

Some of Wisconsin's immigrants cut timber to earn a living.

Many more white settlers moved to Wisconsin in the mid-1800s. Between 1835 and 1850, the population grew from 11,000 to well over 300,000. Lumberjacks chopped down the forests, and farmers cleared away the tree stumps and planted crops. In the second half of the 1800s, Germans, Norwegians, and Poles came from Europe and Canada, and the population quickly passed one million.

These newcomers, called **immigrants**, moved to places in Wisconsin where others from the same country had already settled. Life for the immigrants was easier when their neighbors shared the same language, religion, and customs. As more people from other countries arrived and settled in separate areas, Wisconsin became a patchwork of many ethnic groups.

The immigrants brought new skills to the region, and some found new ways to make a living. Farmers started raising dairy cattle instead of growing wheat, and milk production and cheese-making began. Many factories sprang up in the cities along Lake Michigan. Railroads expanded, and paper mills were built.

On the night of October 8, 1871, the worst fire in Wisconsin's history swept through Peshtigo, killing about 1,000 people. Hundreds of residents jumped into the Peshtigo River for protection. But danger was everywhere. In the river, they had to struggle to keep afloat in water full of people, horses, and cattle.

On the same night, another blaze raged through Chicago in the neighboring state of Illinois, killing only about 200 people. But the Chicago fire got all the attention in the country's newspapers. Few people heard of the Peshtigo fire until the next day, when it was too late to help.

By the 1890s, some of the state's political leaders were thinking about how the government could improve the lives of Wisconsinites. For several decades, the **Republican party** had controlled the government. But many Republicans used their power unfairly, carefully protecting their own interests in the lumber and railroad businesses.

Some Wisconsinites were unhappy with the government of Wisconsin. They decided to split away from the Republicans and form their own branch within the Republican party.

Headed by a man named Robert M. La Follette, Sr., the new program was called **Progressivism,**

The speeches of Robert M. La Follette, Sr., captivated his audience at a county fair in 1897 *(left)*. His wife, Belle Case La Follette, speaks to farmers *(above)*. Mrs. La Follette worked to gain women the right to vote.

because it followed progressive, or new, ideas. The Progressives wanted to give more power to the people. They thought all Wisconsinites—not just a few—should have a say in how the economy worked.

In 1900 La Follette was elected **governor** of Wisconsin. Nicknamed "Fighting Bob," La Follette and the Progressives guided the state through many big changes. New state laws required factory owners to make their companies safer places to work. If a worker got hurt on the job, the company had to pay the doctor's fees. Other laws kept the price of railroad tickets from increasing too rapidly.

Fighting Bob went to Washington, D.C., for 19 years to represent Wisconsin as a **senator** in the U.S. Congress. In 1924 La Follette ran for president of the country as the Progressive party candidate, but he lost the election. Support for the Progressives declined after La Follette's death in 1925.

The 1930s were hard for people across the whole country. Known as the Great Depression, this period left many people short of money, food, and other necessities. Wisconsinites turned again to the Progressive party to solve their problems.

During the depression, La Follette's son Philip served as governor of Wisconsin. The younger La Follette tried to fix some of the state's problems by giving factory workers more power in the workplace and by helping farmers pay their bills. Philip also helped support people who had lost their jobs. He created new jobs by starting projects such as building roads.

Throughout the late 1800s and early 1900s, railroads were built in Wisconsin.

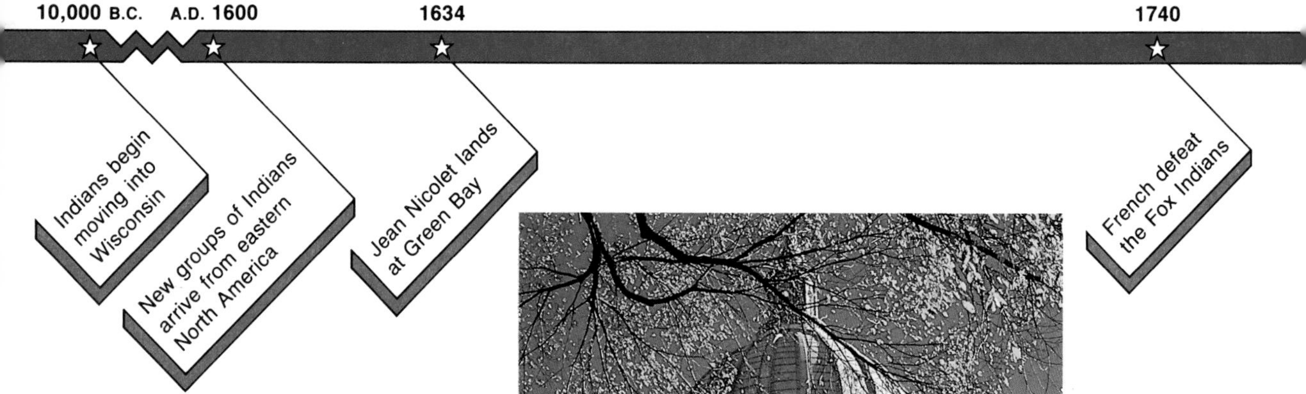

10,000 B.C. A.D. 1600   1634   1740

Indians begin
moving into
Wisconsin

New groups of Indians
arrive from eastern
North America

Jean Nicolet lands
at Green Bay

French defeat
the Fox Indians

**Many historic decisions
and progressive ideas
have been formed at
Wisconsin's state capitol,
located in Madison.**

40

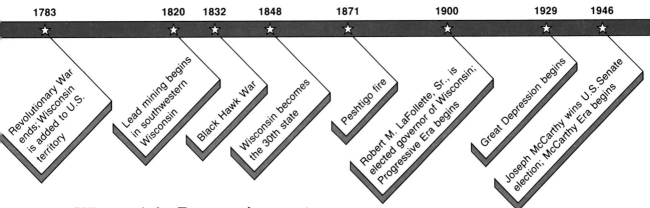

| 1783 | 1820 | 1832 | 1848 | 1871 | 1900 | 1929 | 1946 |

Revolutionary War ends; Wisconsin is added to U.S. territory

Lead mining begins in southwestern Wisconsin

Black Hawk War

Wisconsin becomes the 30th state

Peshtigo fire

Robert M. LaFollette, Sr., is elected governor of Wisconsin; Progressive Era begins

Great Depression begins

Joseph McCarthy wins U.S. Senate election; McCarthy Era begins

Wisconsin's Progressive party died out in 1946, when Joseph McCarthy, a Republican, won the state's election for U.S. senator. McCarthy was concerned that **communists** were beginning to fill government jobs. His followers called him a patriot, but others said he falsely accused workers of disloyalty to the United States. In the end, McCarthy was not able to prove his charges.

Since the McCarthy Era, Wisconsinites who believe in Progressive ideals have usually joined the **Democratic party,** and the state government has shifted between Democratic and Republican control.

41

Living and Working in Wisconsin

Since the arrival of the first Europeans, Wisconsin's population has shifted from being nearly all Indian to nearly all white. Most Wisconsinites today were born in the United States, but their ancestors came from many lands. People from Britain, Germany, Scandinavia, Italy, and Eastern Europe settled in Wisconsin during the 1800s and early 1900s.

Blacks, who make up about 4 percent of the state's population, have come to Wisconsin primarily since the 1940s. More recently, Hispanics and Asians have moved to the state.

Of the state's nearly five million people, fewer than 1 percent—that is, fewer than 50,000—are Native Americans. Many of the Indians live on **reservations**—areas of land that are reserved for a specific tribe. Residents of the reservations have their own government and enforce their own laws.

Two-thirds of the state's people live in cities, and half of these city-dwellers live in Milwaukee, Wisconsin's largest city (population 636,300). Most big communities—including Milwaukee, Madison (the capital), Green Bay, Racine, and Appleton—are located in the southern half of the state.

Milwaukee and Madison are the main cultural centers in Wisconsin. Orchestras, ballets, theater groups, and many museums attract both Wisconsinites and visitors. Students take field trips to museums that specialize in ships, railroads, and circuses as well as in art, history, and natural science.

Many of the buildings in Milwaukee and other places are like

Al's Run, named after the man who started the race, winds down a street in Milwaukee.

Sixth-grade students work through some textbook exercises with the aid of their teacher.

museums. Their architecture—that is, the style in which they are built—tells us about the history of the state. Some of these buildings were designed in the early 1900s by Frank Lloyd Wright, one of the most famous designers of buildings in the United States.

Wisconsin began offering free education in 1845, when its first public elementary school opened. A public high school began operating four years later. In 1856 Margaretta Schurz set up the first kindergarten in the United States at Watertown, Wisconsin.

Wisconsinites are loyal fans of their professional sports teams, including the Green Bay Packers (above) **and the Milwaukee Bucks** (left).

With three professional athletic teams, Wisconsin is a great state for sports fans. Thousands of Wisconsinites cheer on the Green Bay Packers during the football season. Wisconsin's baseball team is the Milwaukee Brewers, and the Milwaukee Bucks play basketball.

In addition, Wisconsin hosts auto races and the American Birkebeiner cross-country ski race. One of the state's most unusual sporting events is a race held in Madison each year—the boats are made from milk cartons!

The City Centre Classic, a bike race held in Appleton, draws hundreds of enthusiastic bikers.

Wisconsin hosts the World Cup Kayak Races in Wausau.

Paper is wound onto huge rolls at a paper mill.

The forests of Wisconsin supply a large paper industry, and many people in the lower Fox River valley and the upper Wisconsin River valley work in paper mills. In fact, Wisconsinites make about 12 percent of the paper used in the United States. The mills also produce paper boxes, tissue paper, and cardboard.

Food processing jobs—for example, making dairy products, canning fruits and vegetables, brewing beer, and packing meat—are also important in Wisconsin. Many of the state's food products are sold in other states.

Most of the money earned in Wisconsin comes from service jobs. This type of work includes jobs in

Nearly one-fourth of all Wisconsinites work in factories. Workers in Milwaukee and other cities in the east make equipment such as engines, ships, tractors, bulldozers, and batteries.

banking, government, schools, and restaurants. Only 2 percent of all the money earned in Wisconsin comes from farming. But when all 50 states are ranked according to yearly income from agriculture, Wisconsin is usually among the top 10.

Workers check the progress of beer brewing in huge kettles.

Some of Wisconsin's farmers grow apples.

Most of the state's farms are located in the south and the east—areas that have the richest soil and the longest growing season. Dairying is the most important type of farming. Nicknamed America's Dairyland, Wisconsin produces more milk than any other state in the country. Some of the milk is processed into butter, cheese, or ice cream at plants throughout the state.

Along roadsides, signs advertise "Cheese" and "Cheese Curds" for sale at local stores and restaurants.

No wonder, since Wisconsin makes about one-third of the cheese produced in the country. The state also produces one-fourth of the nation's butter.

Some farmers raise beef cattle, hogs, and chickens. These animals are sold to meat-packing plants in Milwaukee, Madison, and Green Bay, where they are butchered and packaged for market. Throughout the state, farmers grow hay, corn, and oats to feed livestock.

Most of the vegetable crops—including peas, beets, beans, cabbages, cucumbers, potatoes, and sweet corn—are sent to factories for canning. Some farmers grow fruits such as cranberries, strawberries, raspberries, and apples.

Cranberries are harvested in September.

Both visitors and residents enjoy vivid fall colors (above) **and fishing on Wisconsin's many lakes** (left).

People from other states travel to Wisconsin year-round to enjoy the state's natural beauty. Skiing, hiking, fishing, and swimming are a few of the popular outdoor activities that vacationers like. The money these tourists spend adds to Wisconsin's earnings.

Mining and fishing were once big businesses in Wisconsin, but today they bring in only a small amount of the state's total earnings. Wis-

Lights from a ship docked in Green Bay's harbor sparkle in the night.

consin's miners dig sand, gravel, stone, and lime for use in construction. Those who make their living from fishing operate mostly on Lake Michigan.

Superior, Milwaukee, and Green Bay are busy port cities on the Great Lakes. The harbors receive many products—such as coal, which is used to create electricity for homes and businesses around the state. And from these ports, dairy products, grain, machinery, and other goods made in Wisconsin are shipped throughout the country and overseas.

Door County is noted for the beauty of its forests.

Protecting the Environment

With abundant soil, water, timber, fish, and wildlife, Wisconsin has a wealth of natural resources. Special care must be taken of these treasures, however, if they are to last. One natural resource that many Wisconsinites are concerned about is **groundwater**—the water below the surface of the earth.

Kids such as these *(upper right)* **who are exploring a creek may one day take on the challenges of cleaning polluted streams** *(above).*

Pollution—shot into the air from smokestacks at Wisconsin's paper mills and other factories—eventually falls onto land and water.

Pollution has already made much of the state's surface water (lakes and rivers) unsafe to drink. Most of Wisconsin's supply of drinking water now comes from groundwater, but this water supply can also become polluted.

Farmers spray pesticides on their fields to control insects, weeds, and other pests. They use fertilizers to make crops grow better. Many of these chemicals are very powerful and can be harmful to the environment. Eventually, they may seep through the soil and pollute groundwater.

56

Another threat to groundwater is the disposal of garbage in leaky landfills (places where trash is buried). As the garbage rots and rainwater soaks through, a liquid called **leachate** forms. If the landfill has not been properly sealed, the leachate—which contains harmful materials—will sink farther and contaminate groundwater.

Leaking is not the only problem with Wisconsin's landfills. Another problem is the large amount of garbage people toss each day. Wisconsin's landfills are filling up—most will be full by the year 2000.

By installing a fence, these workers are helping to stop manure, pesticide, and fertilizer from washing into a nearby stream.

57

As Wisconsinites make an effort to throw away less trash each day, they help keep their landfills from overflowing like this one.

Cutting down on the amount of trash thrown away is one way to protect the environment. The Wisconsin Department of Natural Resources (DNR) encourages people to buy items that have less packaging and to reuse things until they are worn out. Some materials, such as plastic and rubber, are so tough that they do not break down even after they are thrown away.

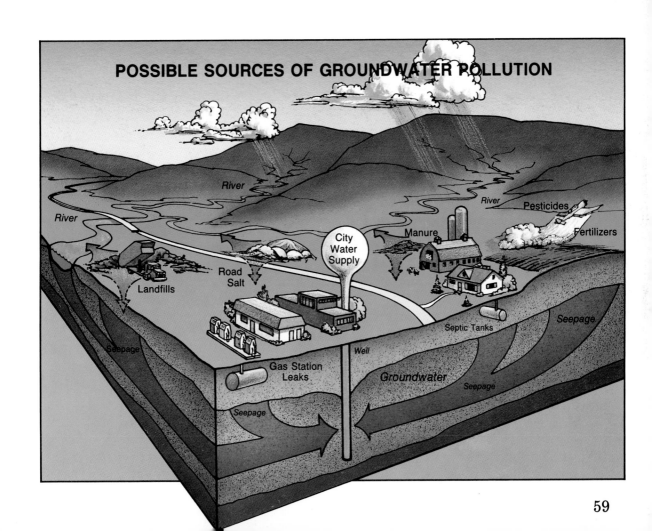

POSSIBLE SOURCES OF GROUNDWATER POLLUTION

River

River

River

Pesticides

Fertilizers

City
Water
Supply

Manure

Landfills

Road
Salt

Septic Tanks

Seepage

Seepage

Gas Station
Leaks

Well

Groundwater

Seepage

Seepage

59

Another way to protect the environment and conserve space in Wisconsin's landfills is to recycle. Recycling is the collection and reprocessing of materials for reuse. Paper, glass jars, metal cans, plastic containers, tires, and oil are some of the products that Wisconsin recycles. Each person in the state can participate in the recycling program by separating articles that can be recycled from the rest of his or her garbage.

Wisconsin has made new laws to protect the environment against waste from factories. Some com-

People of all ages can participate in Wisconsin's recycling efforts.

By protecting the environment, Wisconsinites preserve their state's natural beauty.

pany owners, however, do not want to change. Updated equipment creates less pollution, but it also costs a lot of money. And some business leaders say that the waste their companies create is not really that dangerous.

Other factory owners are more willing to cooperate and have already followed the new laws. If every person and company in Wisconsin tries to help protect the environment, the state can be a clean, healthy place to live.

Wisconsin's Famous People

ACTIVISTS

Zona Gale (1874–1938) was born in Portage, Wisconsin. A writer, Gale supported women's rights, progressive political ideas, and racial equality. She was awarded the Pulitzer Prize in 1921, when her novel *Miss Lulu Bett* was performed as a play.

Ezekiel Gillespie (1818–1892) was probably born a slave. By 1852 he was living in Milwaukee. Gillespie helped win the right to vote for blacks in Wisconsin. He also helped found the first African Methodist Episcopal Church in Milwaukee.

▲ EZEKIEL GILLESPIE

ACTORS

Spencer Tracy (1900–1967) was born in Milwaukee. Tracy won Academy Awards as best actor in the films *Captain Courageous* and *Boys Town*.

Daniel J. Travanti (born 1940) spent his early years in Kenosha, Wisconsin. An actor, Travanti starred in the television series "Hill Street Blues."

Gene Wilder (born 1935), known as Jerry Silberman in his hometown of Milwaukee, is a comedian whose films include *Young Frankenstein* and *Willie Wonka and the Chocolate Factory*.

▲ SPENCER TRACY

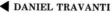 DANIEL TRAVANTI   GENE WILDER

62

ARTISTS

Harry Houdini (1874–1926) was born Erich Weiss in Hungary. A magician who grew up in Appleton, Wisconsin, Houdini was one of the most accomplished escape artists of all times. He also starred in many silent films.

Georgia O'Keefe (1887–1986), born in Sun Prairie, Wisconsin, is one of the nation's best-known artists. She is noted for a series of close-up paintings of flowers, skulls, deserts, and crosses.

Frank Lloyd Wright (1867–1959) was a world-famous architect. Born in Richland Center, Wisconsin, he designed houses and other buildings to blend into their surrounding landscape, often using materials found in the area.

HARRY HOUDINI ▶

CURLY LAMBEAU ▼

ATHLETES

Earl ("Curly") Lambeau (1898–1965) was a professional football coach. As the founder and coach of the Green Bay Packers, Lambeau helped start the National Football League (NFL) in 1921.

Vince Lombardi (1913–1970) coached the Green Bay Packers from 1959 to 1968. During this time, the professional football team won five NFL titles and the first two Super Bowl competitions.

EXPLORERS

John Muir (1838–1914) was born in Marquette County, Wisconsin. A naturalist and explorer, Muir helped found the Sierra Club and promoted the development of national parks and forests.

Jean Nicolet (1598–1642) was a French explorer. In 1634 Nicolet became the first European known to have seen Lake Michigan. He explored Green Bay, the Fox River, and most of the Wisconsin River.

MUSICIANS

Woodrow ("Woody") Herman (1913–1987), originally from Milwaukee, was a leading jazz musician and bandleader during the "big band" days of the 1930s and 1940s.

Wladziu Valentino Liberace (1919–1987) was born in West Allis, Wisconsin. A pianist who performed on television and on stages across the country, Liberace played showy versions of classical and modern music.

▲ WLADZIU LIBERACE

WOODY HERMAN ▶

POLITICIANS & LEADERS

Black Hawk (1767–1838) was a Sauk Indian leader who tried to stop white settlers from taking over lands in Wisconsin and Illinois. In 1838 the U.S. Army defeated him in the Battle of Bad Axe, during the Black Hawk War.

◀ BLACK HAWK

64

Robert Marion La Follette, Sr. (1855–1925), was born in Primrose, Wisconsin. Nicknamed Fighting Bob, La Follette founded the Progressive political party in 1904. He served as governor of Wisconsin from 1901 to 1905 and as U.S. senator from 1906 to 1925. As the Progressive party candidate for U.S. president in 1924, La Follette won 17 percent of the nation's vote.

Joseph Raymond McCarthy (1908–1957) was born in Grand Chute, Wisconsin. As a U.S. senator from 1947 to 1957, McCarthy attacked people he thought were suspicious in any way by calling them communists. McCarthy's wide accusations and harsh methods have come to be known as "McCarthyism."

Oshkosh (1795–1858), a Menominee Indian, led his people in a successful attempt to keep their tribal lands in Wisconsin. As a result of his efforts, the federal government granted the first Menominee reservation. The city of Oshkosh is named after him.

◄ ROBERT LA FOLLETTE, SR.

▲ JOSEPH McCARTHY

▲ OSHKOSH

WRITERS

Marguerite Henry (born 1902), originally from Milwaukee, is the author of *Misty of Chincoteague, Justin Morgan Had a Horse,* and other classic children's books about life with horses.

Laura Ingalls Wilder (1867–1957), born in Pepin, Wisconsin, wrote *Little House on the Prairie* and other stories about her childhood. The books were adapted into a long-running television series.

◄ MARGUERITE HENRY

Facts-at-a-Glance

Nickname: Badger State
Song: "On, Wisconsin"
Motto: Forward
Flower: wood violet
Tree: sugar maple
Bird: robin
Fish: muskellunge (muskie)

Population: 4,808,000 (1990 estimate)
Rank in population, nationwide: 17th
Area: 56,200 sq mi (145,558 sq km)
Rank in area, nationwide: 26th
Date and ranking of statehood:
  May 29, 1848, the 30th state
Capital: Madison
Major cities (and populations*):
  Milwaukee (605,090), Madison (175,830),
  Green Bay (93,470), Racine (82,440),
  Kenosha (74,960)
U.S. senators: 2
U.S. representatives: 9
Electoral votes: 11

*1986 estimates

Places to visit: Cave of the Mounds between Mt. Horeb and Blue Mounds, Circus World Museum in Baraboo, Door County on Door Peninsula, Old World Wisconsin near Eagle, Wisconsin Dells

Annual events: Walleye Weekend in Fond du Lac (June), Holland Festival in Cedar Grove (July), Lumberjack World Championship in Hayward (July), Summerfest in Milwaukee (July), Holiday Folk Fair in Milwaukee (Nov.)

Natural resources: fertile soil, forests, lakes and rivers, sand and gravel, iron, lead, zinc, sulfide, basalt, clay, peat, sandstone

Agricultural products: milk, beef cattle, hogs, chickens, hay, oats, potatoes, sweet corn, beets, green peas, snap beans, cranberries, tart cherries, apples, soybeans, wheat, barley

Manufactured goods: machinery, food products, paper products, electrical equipment, metal products, transportation equipment

ENDANGERED SPECIES
Mammals—Canada lynx, pine martin, timber wolf
Birds—common tern, Forster's tern, piping plover, osprey, peregrine falcon, bald eagle, barn owl
Reptiles—ornate box turtle, queen snake, western ribbon snake, northern ribbon snake, massasauga rattlesnake
Fish—gravel chub, striped shiner, slender madtom, starhead topminnow
Plants—purple milkweed, wild petunia, lake cress, moonwort, floating marsh marigold, beak grass, great white lettuce, small skullcap, sand violet

WHERE WISCONSINITES WORK
Services—51 percent
  (services includes jobs in trade; community, social, & personal services; finance, insurance, & real estate; transportation, communication, & utilities)
Manufacturing—24 percent
Government—15 percent
Agriculture—7 percent
Construction—3 percent

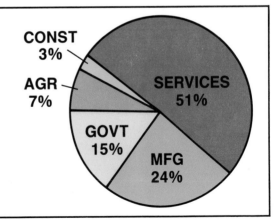

CONST 3%
AGR 7%
SERVICES 51%
GOVT 15%
MFG 24%

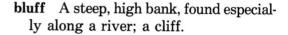

PRONUNCIATION GUIDE

La Follette (la FAHL-et)

Menominee (muh-NAH-muh-nee)

Milwaukee (mihl-WAU-kee)

Mississippi (mihs-uh-SIHP-ee)

Jean Nicolet (zhawn nee-koh-LAY)

Ojibwa (oh-JIHB-way)

Peshtigo (PESH-tih-goh)

Potawatomi (paht-uh-WAHT-uh-mee)

Progressivism (pruh-GRES-ihv-ihzm)

Racine (ruh-SEEN)

Saint Croix (saynt-KRAWee)

Winnebago (wihn-nuh-BAY-goh)

bluff A steep, high bank, found especially along a river; a cliff.

communist A person who believes in communism, a system of government in which the state (rather than private individuals) owns and controls all farms, factories, and businesses.

Democratic party One of the two major political parties in the United States.

glacier A large body of ice that moves slowly over land.

governor The person elected to be head of a state in the United States.

groundwater Water that lies beneath the earth's surface. The water comes from rain and snow that seeps through soil into the cracks and other openings in rocks. Groundwater supplies wells and springs.

ice age A time when glaciers covered a large part of the earth. The term *Ice Age* usually refers to the most recent one, called the Pleistocene, which began almost 2 million years ago and ended about 10,000 years ago.

immigrant A person who moves into a foreign country and settles there.

leachate Liquid formed by the decomposition of waste in a landfill.

missionary A person sent out by a religious group to spread its beliefs to other people.

moraine A mass of sand, gravel, rocks, etc. pushed along or left by a glacier.

Progressivism A political movement that favors new ideas and change in government for the purpose of improving the conditions in which people live and work.

Republican party One of the two major political parties in the United States.

reservation Public land set aside by the government to be used by Native Americans.

senator A member of the Senate, which is one of the two elected groups that makes laws for the United States.

treaty An agreement between two or more groups, usually having to do with peace or trade.

Index ▬▬▬▬▬▬▬▬▬▬▬▬▬▬▬▬▬▬▬▬▬▬▬▬▬▬▬▬▬▬▬▬▬▬